Blaze

FINDS THE TRAIL

by C. W. ANDERSON

Aladdin Paperbacks

New York London Toronto Sydney Singapore

To JOHNNY KEAN
and his pony, *Grasshopper*

Billy was a little boy who had a fine pony named Blaze. Billy loved his pony very much and spent most of his time with Blaze. They went for long rides every day. Billy would often go down to the pasture to pet Blaze.

"You are the finest pony in all the world," he would say. He felt sure it was so.

They rode for some distance over roads they both knew very well. They walked down the hills, so Blaze would not stumble and hurt himself, and then trotted or galloped when they got to the bottom. Soon they were many miles from home.

One day Billy's mother made some sandwiches for him, because he and Blaze were going for a very long ride. They were going to explore an old road through the woods that no one ever used any more. This was exciting. Blaze seemed to enjoy the ride as much as Billy.

They came to the place where the old road turned off, straight into the deep woods. Although it was overgrown with grass and weeds, Billy could still see the deep ruts wagons had made in the ground many years ago. He wanted to see where they would take them.

A beautiful bird, with bright-colored feathers, flew up just in front of them, and the whirr of its wings gave both Billy and Blaze a start. It was a pheasant. Billy had never seen one so close before. He thought it was the most beautiful bird he had ever seen.

A little farther on they saw something red steal quickly across the road.

"It's a fox," cried Billy. "Oh, aren't you glad we came this way, Blaze?"

Blaze seemed to nod his head as he trotted on.

They came to a place where a dead tree was leaning across the road. There was barely room for Blaze to go under it. Billy had to lie flat on Blaze's back, and they just squeezed through.

Then they came to a fallen tree across the road, but Blaze was a fine jumper and sailed over it easily.

"It was a hurricane that blew the tree down." said Billy. "I wouldn't want to be under it when it fell, would you, Blaze?"

They had gone a long way, when Billy saw another big tree across the path. The branches held it up, so that it was too high to jump and too low to go under. Billy hated to turn back when they had come so far.

"Let's try to go around it, Blaze," said Billy. "There must be some way to do it."

The woods were very thick, and each time they tried to get back to the path there were fallen trees or thick woods in the way. They were getting farther and farther from the old road, and still they could not find any opening.

At last they were able to turn back toward the road. Now Billy felt that everything was going to be all right. But they had not gone far before they came to a very deep gully. Billy's heart sank, for he knew they could never get down such a place. They would have to go back again and try a different way. Billy had to lead his pony, for the woods were too thick for him to ride.

There was nothing in sight but woods, and Billy began to be worried. Which way was the road? When he looked for the sun to find what direction he should go, he saw that the sky had become very dark and stormy. It looked very strange, and he was a little frightened. They must get home before the storm.

Billy told Blaze to stand quietly, and he climbed high up in a tall tree. He hoped he might see something that would tell him where they were, but all he could see were treetops everywhere.

"We'll get out somehow," he said to Blaze. He did not want Blaze to know how worried he was.

On they went in the direction Billy felt must be right. The ground was soft and muddy, and suddenly they sank deep in a hole. Billy scrambled out and pulled as hard as he could on the reins. At last Blaze climbed out, covered with mud and looking very frightened. It had been a close call, for the mud hole was very deep.

It was growing very dark and still they could find no sign of a road. Billy was tired and frightened. He knew they were lost. He sat down to rest. Blaze rubbed his soft nose against Billy as if to say, "Don't worry, I'll take care of you." But now a strong wind was blowing, and the sky was very dark and strange looking.

When Billy got up, Blaze started off pulling Billy with him. He seemed to know just where he wanted to go, so Billy followed him.

"Do you really know the way, Blaze?" he cried. "If you only get us out of these woods, I'll give you carrots and sugar every day. Lots and lots of them."

Blaze went right on, dodging around rocks and trees, but always going the same direction.

Suddenly, through the bushes, Billy saw something that made him very happy. It was only an old stone wall, but now he knew they were on the right track. His father had often told how the early settlers had built these walls, with stones they cleared from the land. And where there were walls, there had once been fields and roads leading to them.

Then just ahead he saw an opening in the wall, and a path leading ahead.

"You are wonderful, Blaze!" he cried, "You've found the way."

Now at last he could get in the saddle again, and they could go faster. The wind was growing stronger, and he knew the woods were no place to be in a storm.

They went at a gallop, for the wind was roaring through the treetops and the sky was very black. Suddenly they heard a loud crack, and Blaze leaped forward just as a big dead tree crashed down in the path behind them. "This must be another hurricane." Billy shouted to Blaze. "We'll have to race or we'll never get home."

Blaze was galloping as hard as he could, and Billy was dodging the low branches when he saw, just ahead of them, a wide road. Nothing had ever looked so wonderful to him. Now he knew that home was just a mile down the road.

"You did it!" Billy shouted in Blaze's ear as the wind howled around them. "You're a wonderful pony!"

They could see the lights of home, and Blaze was really flying. He wanted to be in his nice snug stable, away from this wild storm. The air was full of leaves and flying branches torn from the trees.

"Just a little farther and we'll be there," cried Billy. He knew that Blaze was very tired, but he still kept on as fast as he could go.

Billy's father was out in the road when they galloped up to the house. He was very happy to see them safe, and he called to Billy's mother to tell her the good news. He told Billy that this was really a hurricane, and they had been worried about him. He went down to the stable to help Billy dry off Blaze.

"As soon as you are rested and cooled off, I'll give you a wonderful dinner." Billy said to Blaze as he rubbed his pony's wet shiny coat. "He found the way out of the woods." he told his father.

"He's a fine pony," said Billy's father.

"He's the best pony in all the world," cried Billy.

"I think so too," said his father.